TALES FROM THE FESTIVAL HALL

Nick Yapp

Nick Yapp

***i*
Imprimata**

Published by **Imprimata**

Copyright © Nick Yapp 2008
Nick Yapp has asserted his rights under the Copyright Designs
and Patents Act 1988 to be identified as the author of this work.
All rights reserved. No part of this publication may be reproduced,
stored in or introduced into a retrieval system or transmitted in
any form or by any means (electronic, mechanical or otherwise
and whether invented now or subsequently) without the prior
written permission of the publisher or be otherwise circulated
in any form, other than that in which it is published, without a
similar including this condition being imposed on any subsequent
publisher. Any person who does any unauthorized act in relation to
this publication may be liable to criminal
prosecution and civil action.

A CIP Catalogue record for this book is available
from the British Library

ISBN 978-1-906192-26-6

Set in 11½pt Minion Pro (InDCS3)

Printed in Great Britain

i

Imprimata

Imprimata Publishers Limited
50 Albemarle Street, London W1S 4BD.

Contents

The Piano Shifter's Tale
    Ars Longa 7

The Bassoonists's Tale
    The Buffoon's Awakening 19

The Busker's Tale
    Just A Dream 33

The Critic's Tale
    The Evil Transcribers. 47

The Nerd's Tale
    Toscanini's Foot 61

The Concertgoer's Tale
    Spell-Bound Love 75

The Piano Shifter's Tale

Ars Longa

He was so rich. You must have read about him in the papers… must have! I mean, this guy was fabulously wealthy. He tried to keep it quiet, of course – don't they all – didn't want the world to know. Kept all his big spending private. Bought things under assumed names. I mean, not just paintings and jewellery and antiques and all that – this guy bought houses, villages, whole islands, he was so rich. He bought cars like you and me buy chocolate bars. He bought boats, helicopters, private jets. Tell you how rich he was – he bought a village in India and had it moved to Portugal. He liked the place, you see, and wanted to visit it more often – like, for breakfast. But India's too far away for breakfast, so he made them move it to the Algarve. He could get to the Algarve in an hour and a half – in one of his jets.

He liked the good things in life – good food, good wine, good air. He paid millions having his chateau in France covered in a glass dome a quarter of a mile in diameter, just so he could breathe purified air. He had the old air pumped out of the dome and fresh air pumped in. Lavender perfumed. From Provence. And he liked good clothes. He'd spend what would have been a year's wages to you and me on a tie – you know, wild silk with crushed diamonds held together by gold thread.

Now, I didn't say he had good taste. You can't have that much money and power and good taste. Not possible. I mean, what he called 'good music', you and me would have turned our noses up at. Light music. I mean, music so light it practically flew out the window. Music from the Movies, Love Themes from Cable TV, Great Hits of the Hospital Wards, the LSO Plays the Best Advertising Jingles of All Time – that sort of stuff. Wept when he heard it. I saw him – with my own eyes. The day it happened. Just before the end.

I was working at the Festival Hall. On the South Bank. Not a bad place, even since they've tarted it up. Not a bad gig, either. Behind the scenes stuff. Setting up exhibitions in the foyer, slinging out old furniture, putting in new, and moving the grand piano across the stage when she was having an outing for a concert. You know, they play an overture, and then it's the old Joanna concerto. Out we come – Larry, Mo and me – move the fiddle desks, shove the Naughty Forte across the stage, and then manoeuvre her into position. Front, centre stage. Stop. Brakes on the casters. Quick look at the positioning. Brakes off. Fiddle fiddle. Brakes on. Then put the desks back and away we go. And when we get to the storage space at the side, out of sight of the audience, we always turn to each other – Larry and Mo and me – and we all sing 'I did it Steinway…!' Silly. But there you are.

And then we have the concerto. Mozart 21, that's my favourite, and back we come and do the whole exercise in reverse, taking Naughty Forte back home.

So that's why I was there, the night it happened. This guy, this fabulously rich guy, had booked the Hall for a concert. The whole Hall. Just for himself. No one else was allowed in – private function. He was the entire audience. Fifth row stalls. Row E, Seat 27. Best seat in the house for a piano concerto – bit to the *side*, you see, so he could clock the pianist's fingers flashing up and down the keys.

Who's playing? The Chicago Philharmonic. Who's paying? The rich guy. Imagine it – flying in an entire orchestra, eighty seven players – just for a single concert with an audience of one. Plus the technicians and the music librarian, and the agent, and the manager, and a whole crowd of musical hangers-on. Who's conducting? Maestro Conrad von Dahrendorf. What's it cost to have his services for a night? Fifty thousand quid me and Larry reckon – which is nothing to this guy. Peanuts. Like the price of a cinema ticket for you and me.

And who's going to play Rachmaninoff's Joanna Concerto Number 2 in C Minor? Sylvie Maurois. The doyenne of pianists. Sixty, if she's a year. Built like a Regimental Sergeant Major. Temper like a pit bull, so they say. But what a talent! What a touch! You'd have thought the keys were made of liquid gold the way she could make a melody flow. And, of course, old Rachman's Number 2 is stuffed with melody. That last movement. Glorious. All the power of cheap music, and all the weight and wonder of the classical. Fantastic. Mo and me used to call it the Kleenex Koncerto… but that was before the night I'm telling you about.

And the icing on the cake, the grand finale of the whole absurd evening was going to be Tchaikovsky 6. The

Pathétique. That's another one to get you going, that is. So, all in all, it promised to be an emotional night. But none of us guessed how emotional.

I saw it all. From the word 'go'. Heard the guys from Chicago limbering up in the band room. Saw Sylvie sweep in with her maid and her hairdresser and her masseuse and her manager. Opened the door myself for Maestro von Dahrendorf.

Seven thirty, we were all ready. Orchestra on stage, paraded in their white polo necks - a gift from the rich guy - and DJs, tuned up, ready to do battle with *Fingal's Cave*. Ushers on all the doors – fire regulations, you see… don't matter how many's in… got to make sure no one puts a coat on the landing rail. Maestro waiting in the wings. Sylvie sipping a can of Coke in her dressing room. Larry, Mo and me sharing a few cans of lager, all ready to get Naughty Forte in place when the time comes.

But where's his nibs? Where's Mr Moneybags? Not there. Five minutes… ten minutes… in he comes. No apology, doesn't even look at the orchestra. Ushered to his seat. No thanks to anyone – I didn't say he had good *manners*, did I? Sits down. Fusses with his clothes. Has a good cough. Then signals he wants them to begin.

You could tell the Maestro didn't like that, from the way he walked on. Very slow – in total silence. No applause from the rich guy. It was all so weird, and I got this feeling we were in for an odd night. Odd? That's putting it mildly.

Anyway… Maestro taps on his desk. Up go the fiddle sticks, and we're off. The way those guys from Chicago played! Magic. You know, you can hear music like that over and over again and you think you're tired of it, but when you get a top band like that, playing at their best, it's pure bloody magic. Felt the hair go up on the back of my neck. Larry and Mo and me nodded at each other. Mo muttered: 'We're in for a treat tonight.'

Seven minutes later, the overture's finished. Total silence. The rich guy doesn't even clap. Nobody knows what to do. Maestro doesn't bow, doesn't signal to the band to rise – well, he couldn't, could he. I mean, you can't acknowledge total silence. Maestro goes off. Larry, Mo and me wait to see if he's coming on again – but of course he's not. No point. No applause.

So we swing Naughty Forte across the stage to front centre. Stop. Twiddle her round and about. Brakes on. Lid up. Off we go. But out of the corner of my eye I copped a look at the rich guy. And I could swear he was crying.

Now – you could feel the tension in the atmosphere. You know how the guys in the band usually chat quietly to each other in between numbers? Not a word. Leader goes up to Naughty Forte. Hits 'A'. Everyone retunes. Leader motions for quiet. Slight pause. On comes Maestro with Sophie. And she's wearing this knockout gown. It's like an exploding rose – deep red, very fussy and flamboyant. And it's saying very loudly: 'I am an *artiste*… a performer… a star…'

Over she goes. Sits on the stool, nods to Maestro – and off we go again. First movement ends. Not a sound. On we go. Second movement. And in the quietest passage – which Sylvie is playing like a dream – the rich guy starts coughing. And there's something about his coughing. Like… he's flaunting it. Like… it's deliberate. Larry and Mo and me were livid, because what Sylvie and the band are coming across with is like nothing you've ever heard before. You felt like you were poised to win a fortune, like the most wonderful thing in your life was about to happen, like nothing could ever go wrong again. And the rich guy's hacking and hawking and spitting in his hankie.

But Sylvie played on. And the guys in the band went right along with her. End of the second movement. Third and last coming up. But the rich guy's still coughing. So the maestro waits. And waits… and waits. We see his face from the side. The sweat's pouring off him and he's beetroot red. I thought he was going to catch fire with anger. But no. Professional, you see. And Sylvie? Well, I reckoned she was aware of nothing but the music. Soaked in it. Lost in it. Locked in it.

At last the rich guy stops coughing, and the Maestro waves the band in for the Third Movement. And it's even better than before. I've never heard playing like it. As though everyone on stage was determined to give the performance of their lives. I couldn't take my eyes off it, but I could hear Mo sobbing…and it wasn't the lager.

When they hit that glorious tune near the end! God, I thought my heart would burst. I lost all sight of where I was – could have been in Heaven. There was just this glorious sound pouring all over me. Right the way through to the finish. Wow!

It wasn't a surprise to hear silence after that. If the place had been full, I doubt that anyone would have clapped. Not straight off. You had to recover first.

And then… from Row E Seat 27, comes this voice.

'Play that last bit again.'

It's not a request. It's an order. And it was like all the

music had gone… completely disappeared. Hadn't ever happened. It was like we were the staff in a restaurant, and a haughty customer was telling us off.

Maestro turned round. Sylvie looked up. The band stared into the auditorium.

'Play that last bit again.'

I couldn't see how Sylvie was taking this, but Maestro found his voice.

'An encore is a privilege an audience has to earn.'

The rich guy ignored him. 'Play that last bit again,' he said, 'and I'll double your fee.'

I heard Larry mutter something about 'that'll set the sod back another 200k…', but it never came to that. Because Sylvie arose with a kind of snarl from her stool, with her fists clenched and waving in the air. Kind of Wagnerian. For a second or two she seemed to be searching around for something, then she snatched the bit of wood that props up the piano lid, and snapped it off. The lid came down with a crash that set all the wires inside it humming this mad chord.

And Sylvie was off, barging through the fiddles, knocking desks over, down the steps at the side of the stage and into the body of the Hall. Nobody else moved. We were all spectators at the appalling event that followed.

She went right up to Row D – the row in front of where this rich guy was sitting – with this stick of wood in her hand – stumbling between the rows until she was right opposite him. I thought she was just going to crack him over the nut. He opened his mouth to say something, and she shoved the stick right into his mouth, through it, and down, into his throat and neck, like she was stabbing him with a sword. And there was this awful bubbling noise and a choking sort of cough, and he staggered upright, and she went on thrusting the stick into him. I think he tried to grab her arm and push her away, but she was too strong for him. And then, suddenly, he crashed down.

We knew he was dead. I don't know how... none of us was within fifty feet of him. But we all knew he was dead. Sylvie stood over him for a moment or two, panting, shaking. Then she slowly made her way back, between the rows, to the curtains at the side, where she collapsed into the arms of her manager and her hairdresser.

Other than that, nobody moved – not one of the eighty-seven guys in the band, not one of the ushers, not the Maestro, not Larry, not Mo, not me.

Then it started. So quiet you could hardly hear it – I think it was one of the first fiddles - started on the opening bars of the Fourth Movement of the *Pathétique*. And another took it up, and then several joined in, and by bar sixteen all the strings were playing, and the Maestro was conducting. It was magnificent. It was terrible. It was... well, the only word for it is 'pathetic', in the true sense of the word.

A couple of the ushers crept forward, but they wouldn't touch the body. And somebody must have phoned for an ambulance, because a few minutes later a couple of paramedics came rushing in. But the band played on. To the end. To those last haunting bars, to that final *diminuendo* that fades so slowly and so gently you can never tell exactly when it's stopped. And the Maestro left the stage, and came back on, and bowed, and motioned the band to stand – just as the paramedics were carrying the body out on a stretcher.

You must have read about his death in the papers. 'Respiratory failure', they said it was. Hushed it all up. Coroner didn't know what to make of it – but no witnesses came forward. Amazing. More than a hundred of us there… and everyone kept their mouths shut. The power of the people…

And you know that Indian village in Portugal? That's a theme park now. And that chateau in France that's all glassed in? That's a holiday centre. But the Tchaikovsky 6? That's still the same. That's still a bloody good piece of music.

The
Bassoonists's Tale

The Buffoon's Awakening

It all started with the tape – the "cassette", as she insists on calling it. We've got this little old cassette player in the bathroom… stupid, really, to keep the thing on, but Felicity and I didn't have the money at first and don't have the time now to replace all the old tapes with CDs. So there it is, in the bathroom. At least, that's where it's supposed to be. I switch it on when I'm shaving in the morning, and last thing at night when I'm brushing my teeth. I used to think that Felicity moved it only when she was going to do some ironing. Now I know better.

It's all very silly really, and yes, I do regret doing what I did. It finished my career with the Manchester Philly, and the only hope I've got left is the chance of the second bassoon chair in Salt Lake City. There's a certain irony there – a guy who reckons he's been cuckolded playing for a load of Mormons.

But I'll tell you about the tape… the "cassette", as Felicity insists on calling it. Felicity and I are often late to bed. By the time a concert's finished and she's put her flute away and I've dismantled the bassoon, we don't get away from any venue much before a quarter to ten – and that's if we haven't stopped to have a gargle with some of the band. So, if the gig's out of town, we might not get home much before midnight. We might watch some late news on TV, five minutes or so. Then she brushes her teeth in the bedroom, using one of those electric brushes. I brush mine by hand, as nature intended, in the bathroom. And so to bed...

Now, even though I'll be making music all day and all night, I still like to start each morning with a song. I shove down the PLAY button, and there's *Simon and Garfunkel*, or the *Fab Four*, or maybe Billy Joel. But, and this started a few weeks ago, all I got every morning was old Fred Astaire. And it was always the same track... in the middle of the tape... Some tune about *Bojangles*. I didn't even know we had an Astaire tape. It was all right, pleasant in its way, and very Thirties. And I want to make it clear that I've got nothing against dear old Fred, or at least, I hadn't then.

But then the tape player (the "cassette player" to Felicity) disappeared for a couple of days. On the third morning, I asked Felicity where it was, and she seemed a bit flustered and said it was in the bedroom. She fetched it, and then looked even more flustered as she snatched the tape out of it.

'I'll get one of yours,' she said.

I thought that was a very odd thing for her to say. We don't have *my* tapes and *her* tapes. We have *our* tapes, or we did have until this Astaire tape came on the scene. That was nothing to do with me. I don't know where it came from or when. And yes, of course, it was the Astaire tape that Felicity grabbed out of the cassette player.

For a week or more the cassette player stayed in the bathroom, and then it disappeared again. Felicity was away that day, doing some school work, so I went looking for it. And in the end, I found it in the bottom of her wardrobe, which I thought was a strange place for it. I pressed PLAY, and there it was again… the song about Bojangles.

So I started wondering, and three questions formed themselves in my mind. One – why had Felicity hidden the cassette player? Two – why all the fuss and secrecy about this Astaire tape? And Three – what was the particular significance of this *Bojangles* number? I thought about it all over the weekend, and right through Monday. The Philly hadn't got any gigs and weren't due to start rehearsals until Tuesday. But I still couldn't come up with any answers to my questions. Felicity could be going mad, but she seemed sane enough… a little more tired than usual, but then we'd just completed a pretty hectic schedule, recording the complete cycle of Beethoven symphonies, including Downing Street, which was the name my co-bassoonist in the Philly gave to Number Ten.

We'd got this new resident conductor, the summer before – William Reno. And he'd set out to make his name straight off by plunging us into a season where we concentrated on all the great German symphonies of the 19th century… Brahms; Schubert; Mahler 1, 2 and 3; and, of course, good old Ludwig.

You may not have come across Boss Reno yet. He's an American, and he's young, pushy, smart, and glamorous in an old fashioned Hollywood way - you know, slight, dapper, bony-faced. As a matter of fact, in his tails he's not unlike Fred Astaire. And I'll confess it here and now - I don't like him.

He drove us hard. He told us he wanted more snap

in our playing, and he got it. Even the critics picked it up: 'Bright new sound and sound new future for the Manchester Philharmonic', one of them wrote. Well, not such a bright new future for me, as it turned out.

When Felicity got back from a school gig that day, I asked her about the tape and she became quite aggressive. She said it was nothing to do with me. Then she seemed to get anxious, and asked me where "the cassette" was, what I'd done with it. I told her I hadn't done anything with it. I told her I had just found it in the cassette player in the wardrobe. The moment I said that, she burst into tears. I tried to comfort her, but she didn't want comfort, and I suppose, if I'm honest, I was holding back a little on the TLC. She must have felt that, too, because she got huffy. She told me she didn't want to talk about it. All she wanted was *her* tape and *her* bed.

The following week the Philly didn't have any concerts. Felicity and I had some more workshop sessions with local schools in the mornings, and rehearsals every afternoon from Tuesday onwards. But on the Tuesday morning, Felicity said she had a splitting headache and couldn't come with me to the school. She hoped she'd be better in time for the rehearsal.

So did I, because both of us knew it was about as important a rehearsal as the Philly had ever had. The critic's initial paeans of praise for Bill Reno had turned to somewhat sour conjecture. They still agreed that he was great on the 19th century repertoire, but wanted to know when concertgoers would get the chance to hear his interpretations of more modern masterpieces? Where were Stravinsky, Szymanowski, Boulez? So Reno had decided he'd have to put his toe into atonal, into the modern masters. Modern! His idea of modern was about as up-to-date as poor old Fred Astaire.

But El Reno had chosen a high profile concert in which to take this "giant" stride forward. We were booked to play the Royal Festival Hall, London... a "Gala Night in the presence of Their Royal Highnesses". The whole shoot was to be televised live on BBC 4. Reno and Giles Brackley, the Orchestra manager, had gone into huddles together for weeks, discussing what we should play. Finally they decided - nothing Germanic, time to take a trip to the Mediterranean... a chance for Reno to show how he handled colour. So we were to do Xenakis's *Terretektorh*, a bit of de Falla as a sop to Their Royal Highnesses, and Milhaud's *La Création du Monde*. And we were going to kick off the evening with some Ravel... the *Pavane pour une infante défunte*, and then *Alborado del Gracioso*. That meant a busy night for me and some tricky showcase stuff for Felicity, which was why I hoped she'd be better in time for the rehearsal.

Well, she was. Just. The rehearsal was due to start at 2.30 in the Town Hall, and she turned up with just two minutes to go. Boss Reno, on the other hand, was twenty minutes late. No band likes that, and it was a bad start to a lousy rehearsal. Horn One had a sod of a time with the opening to the *Pavane*. If he wasn't fluffing the first note, he was cracking on the second. We ploughed on through it, but the magic that should have been there was missing.

Eventually, Reno said we'd have to leave it, and I don't think I was the only one in the band to take that as a nasty insult. Reno wanted to try the other Ravel piece – the

Alborado. Now, there's a very exposed bit of fat there for the bassoon… right at the beginning of the second section It's a bold theme, a kind of young man's assertion of his masculinity… very macho, very Spanish.

I gave it my best shot. I thought it was OK, but it didn't do for Reno.

'Again,' he said. I played it again. Then he said: '…once more.' I played it yet again. Then he told me how I should phrase it. Finally he said we'd come back to it the next day, which is as near as any conductor's ever come to telling me I'm crap. I was livid. When the rehearsal ended and Felicity and I were driving home, I sounded off about Reno. She kept telling me to leave it, but I was far too angry for that. Then she suddenly snapped at me.

'He's a great conductor. He's entitled to demand we play what he wants, how he wants it. You don't know anything about him. He's… he's a wonderful guy.'

Well, well, well.

There was something in her voice that made me shut up. And I started thinking some more.

I was still thinking at rehearsal the following day. The *Pavane* was better. I have to admit that Reno was adept at sorting out Horn One's entry. And he just adored Felicity's playing. She could do no wrong. Her phrasing was beautiful. Her tone was "seductive". Her flutter-tongueing was like 'a humming bee sipping nectar'.

Some of the lads sniggered at that, and Mike, in the heavyweight contra-bassoon chair next to mine, muttered something about: 'He fancies her.' You know what? Even as he said it, I knew he was right.

When the rehearsal ended, Reno beckoned Felicity up to him. She hurried across and they had this happy little *tête à tête*. I watched them as I cleaned out the old *fagotto*. I was more and more certain that Mike was right. They looked like bloody lovers. When Felicity came back to put her flute away, she was all aglow. And she was humming... another old Astaire number. I recognized the tune, though I couldn't put a name to it at the time. It was an old Evergreen from the Thirties. I thought it was by Gershwin, maybe, or perhaps Cole Porter. The thing was, it was definitely an old Astaire number, something he'd danced to with Ginger Rogers. I wondered if it was on that tape.

So that night I waited until Felicity had gone to sleep, and then went looking for the tape. I couldn't find it anywhere – the kitchen, the front room, the attic, under the stairs. I tried everywhere, including the garden shed, and found absolutely no trace of the tape. I found every other tape in the house, but no sign of Fred. I went back to bed in a worse temper than any bassoonist has ever gone to bed in.

But, next day, there it was, right in front of my eyes, in Felicity's flute case. I caught a glimpse of it at rehearsal. That night, I waited for her to go to sleep again. But she kept fussing and reading, until it became clear that *she* was waiting for *me* to go to sleep first. So I pretended I'd dropped off. A few minutes later, she slid out of bed, unhooked her bathrobe from the back of the bedroom door, and crept downstairs. I gave her time to get settled into whatever she wanted to do, and then got up and tiptoed into the spare room, where we keep all our music gear.

I opened her flute case, took out the tape, picked up the cassette player from the bathroom and tiptoed back into the bedroom. It didn't occur to me till later to wonder just what Felicity was doing downstairs.

I got back into bed, plugged in a set of headphones, and pressed PLAY. There it was again, that tune about Bojangles. Then it hit me. If you had a favourite track on a tape, you'd listen to it and *then* you'd stop the tape. You might rewind to hear the track again, but you still wouldn't leave it tee-ed up at the start of your favourite track. You'd leave it at the *end* of your favourite track. So the tune that mattered, the one that was somehow special to Felicity was the one before *Bojangles*. I hit REWIND, counted slowly to sixteen, and then pressed PLAY.

And what did I hear? Right! Astaire singing… *Won't you change partners and dance with me…?* That was the name of the song Felicity had been humming, and suddenly it came to me that it wasn't by Gershwin or Porter. It was by Irving Berlin.

I stopped the tape, shoved the headphones under the pillow, popped the cassette player back in the bathroom, and dropped the tape back into Felicity's flute case. And then I wondered what she was doing. She was on the phone in the kitchen. And she was singing… very, very *pianissimo*. She was singing the same bloody song. And she was laughing…

I knew it all then. She and Reno were having an affair and that was *their* song. He was Fred Astaire and she was Ginger Rogers. God knows who I was supposed to be… But I tell you who I felt like - that dreadful schmuck who was second banana in all their films… Edward Everett Horton.

What did I do? Nothing. What did I say? Nothing. I just let it gnaw away inside me... right through the rest of that week of rehearsals. Right through the bloody *Création du Monde* and the Interlude and Dance from *La Vida Breve*, and Xenakis, and Ravel. Reno worked us hard, and I have to admit, we all got better. He was pleased with us, even more pleased with himself, and he told us how much he was looking forward to the concert on Monday in London.

On Monday afternoon we were all down in the Festival Hall for a last run through before the concert that night. We got the modern stuff out of the way pretty quick – it's my belief that conductors like Reno can't tell if you're playing Xenakis well or not – and then we knocked off the *Pavane*. It was beautiful.

Reno left the *Alborado* till last.

'Let's take a look at that middle passage,' he said, 'which we never seem to get exactly right.'

I knew what was coming. It didn't matter how I played it, he didn't like it. It was too warm, too cold, too pedantic, too raucous, too hesitant, too French.

Out of the corner of his mouth, Mike muttered to me: 'He may fancy your bird, mate – but he don't like you, does he?'

Me, I was pissed off. This had nothing to do with the way I was playing. This was the lover sneering at the cuckold husband. This was the guy who was screwing my wife, shitting on me.

And I sat there and took it. But I promised myself I'd find a way of getting back at him.

Four hours later, we're on stage. The Festival Hall's packed. Their Royal Highnesses are up in the box. We've breezed through the National Anthem – I'll say this for Reno, he didn't hang about on *God Save the Queen*. We've given as good an account of the *Pavane* as I've ever heard, and we're well into the *Alborado*. Felicity is flutter-tongueing for all she's worth. And I suddenly had this thought... I wonder if she does that to Reno? I wonder what they do, and where, and whether either of them – or both – thinks of me...?

Not a good idea to think things like that in the middle of a concert. And my big moment was just coming up. The bit I could never please my sodding master with. We swept into the last few bars of the first section, and there it was – my big solo. I vowed I'd play it like it had never been played. That would show him.

Reno nods in my direction. They're all waiting for me. I took a deep breath, and blew.

It's silly, isn't it, but I still don't know what made me do it. It was the biggest occasion in the history of the band. We were playing to a packed house, with royalty up in the box, all the critics in, and with live TV cameras on the band. Live TV, with the cameras on me. And there's me blowing away into my bassoon and what's coming out isn't Ravel, it's Irving Berlin. I'm playing *Won't you change partners and dance with me*. But the joy of it was, nobody did anything. For what seemed like ages. I blew on and on, and nobody knew what to do. Mike's hissing: 'For Chrissake, knock it off!' But everyone in the Hall is listening with as much attention as you ever get from a gala audience, as though

Ravel actually wrote what I'm playing.

Eventually, Reno did the only thing he could do, and waved the rest of the band in to drown me out. I went along with that. I'd made my point. I'd mucked up his big concert. I'd showed him I knew what he'd been up to. And I'd ruined my career.

Felicity wouldn't speak to me that night. She saved it all up for the morning after. And I discovered I'd been really silly. It turned out that she wasn't having an affair with Reno, that she wouldn't dream of such a thing. She *liked* him, admired him, was flattered by the attention he paid her, but she loved *me*. So much so, that if I do get the job in Salt Lake City, I might even be able to persuade to come out with me.

And the tape? That was something she and Mike had dreamed up for the band party at Christmas. They'd planned to do a Fred and Ginger routine, as a surprise. If I don't get the job in Utah, maybe they'll let me creep in through the back door to see it.

There's just one thing that still bothers me. But no, there couldn't be anything going on between Mike and Felicity. No… of course not… but, then again, you can never be sure, can you…

The Busker's Tale

Just A Dream

You know that old gag where the comic says: 'I was standing in this bus shelter outside the Savoy Hotel this morning… that's where I'm staying at the moment…in the bus shelter outside the Savoy Hotel'? That's me. Only it's not the Savoy, but smack across the river from there. It's the Festival Hall. And that's where I'm playing at the moment…outside the Festival Hall.

I'm a busker…soprano sax, doubling clarinet. That's another old gag…where someone gives the comic a clarinet and he says: 'I can't play this! It's full of holes!' The clarinet…an ill woodwind that nobody blows good. Except dear old Acker. Remember Acker Bilk? *Stranger on the Shore*? Lovely. Specially if you do it with plenty of *vibrato*. The punters love that. And the good old good ones. 'Every time it rains, it rains…pennies from heaven…' And it bloody does rain, too, on the South Bank. Which is one of the reasons why it's always been my ambition to play *inside* the Festival Hall.

And why not? It's not all Ripsiskorsetsov and Page Nine, is it? That's another very old gag. The comic says: 'Ladies and Gentlemen, I'd now like to play for you the Page Nine Violin Concerto', and the feed says 'Page Nine? Page Nine!

That's Paganini, you fool!' No, they do all sorts of things at the Festival Hall. Pop concerts, light music, even the odd Benny Goodman revival night. Now, he *could* play the clarinet. Marvellous.

So, if they let Goodman into Carnegie Hall back in 1938, how about letting yours truly into the Festival Hall. Give my best set of teeth for that, I would. The ones I use for the clarinet. But I didn't have to. Remember that old gag about the bloke in New York who stops a woman on the street and says: 'Can you tell me how to get to Carnegie Hall?' And the woman says: 'Practice.' Well, I'll tell you the best way to get to the Festival Hall. Have the right friends. That's how I made it.

I've got this regular customer. Lovely lady. Sara without an 'h' is her name. Most nights when the weather's fine I see her. In the evening. She passes my pitch on her way home from work. She works just downstream from me, at Capital Television. She's a producer. Doesn't always put money in the box but often stops for a chat. And that's how it all started.

She does this TV series…*Dreams Come True*. You know the one. Ordinary people write in saying what their dreams are, and the programme makes their dreams come true. Only, Sara says the trouble is, either the dreams are too expensive – like this couple who wanted to visit her mum in Jersey on Cunard's *Queen Victoria* and the programme budget wouldn't run to that – or the dreams are just, you know, ridiculous. Like blokes writing in to say they want to play football for England in the World Cup Final, and score the winning goal in the last minute of extra time, with their left foot.

Poor old Sara. *Dreams Come True* is more like a nightmare for her. She says the problem is getting glamorous items on the show that don't cost too much. And that's when I said: 'Well, that rules me out.' And she said 'Why, what's your dream?' And I told her. To play *inside* the Festival Hall.

A week later she was back. Wanted to have a talk with me. No promises, but she had been thinking about how to make my dream come true. What she had in mind was a special *Dreams Come True* concert with the Capital Television Concert Orchestra. I said I didn't know there was such an orchestra, and she said there wasn't, but there would be if her idea came off. She'd even got some thoughts about the music. Obviously the sig tune from the show, and lots of lovely melodies with 'Dream' in the title…everything from *I'll See You in My Dreams* to Mendelssohn's music for *A Midsummer Night's Dream* to Elvis's *If I Can Dream*. And, because Capital TV is a London station, there'd be a special London medley in the middle – all jellied eels and Pearly Kings and Queens and *In Town Tonight* and Indian takeaways and *Old Father Thames* and cancelled trains and the Westminster Chimes.

And that's where I'd come in. Literally. Get my chance to play inside! The medley would be a kind of clarinet concerto, made up of London tunes. I said, 'you mean, like, *A Foggy day in London Town, London Pride, Knocked 'em in the Old Kent Road, Bike up the Strand…*' She said she didn't know that last one. It's a gag, of course. I think it was Gerry Mulligan…rewrote *Strike Up the Band* on the same chords, but called it *Bike up the Strand*. Then I told her about the long history of marriages between classical music and jazz clarinet players. About how Stravinsky wrote the *Ebony Concerto* for Woody Herman, and how Goodman recorded Mozart's *Clarinet Quintet*. Sara asked me if I wanted to borrow her CD of Acker playing the *Kegelstadt Trio* but when I said I didn't mind if I did, she just laughed. Don't ask me why.

Anyway, by now she was really enthusiastic. Her bosses at CTV loved the idea. She said they were committed to staging a certain number of live events in London each year and this would be something new and novel and exciting. How much rehearsal time did I think I'd need with the orchestra? I said, so long as I knew what tunes were going to make up this medley, no time at all. Just a run through. She told me to make a list of all the London songs I knew and liked, and Marcus Urwin would take his pick.

'Who's Marcus Urwin?' I said.

'He's our MD,' she said.

'And he knows about music? Most doctors don't.'

Sara said MD stood for Musical Director, and I felt the South Bank shake as my attempt at a gag hit the concrete.

Anyway, I sent in my list, and waited. And on her weekly stop-by, Sarah told me how things were going. The orchestra was booked…45 pieces…strings, brass, woodwind, even a harp. The Hall was booked. People were busy designing the posters and planning the publicity, and would I come over to the Capital Studios one afternoon for a photo shoot? My picture would be on the posters.

'The London Medley is the highpoint of the concert,' she said. 'You'll be a star. You'll get star billing. You're going to be famous…' Then she laughed and said, 'I don't even know your name.'

'Well,' I said, 'outside the Festival Hall it's Jim Emms. Inside perhaps it ought to be James.'

'No,' said Sara. 'Jim Emms is fine. Our *Dreams Come True* Clarinet Virtuoso. A whole new career beckons, Jim. You're going to be a celebrity. You'll never have to play outside again.'

'That'd be good,' I said. 'Winter's coming. That wind by the river does my *obligato* no good whatsoever.' I was looking forward to a longer chat, but Sara said she had to be off, and could she have my address so that she could send me all the details. I said that she could just drop stuff off as she passed my pitch, but she said she was going to be very busy – 'increasingly busy' was the phrase she used – and wouldn't have time to stop for a chat.

I didn't see her for two or three weeks after that and wondered if the whole concert idea was off. But then I got a note from Sara's assistant – someone called Trixie Ayres – inviting me to Capital Studios to have me picture taken. I turned up good and early, looking my best, and waited in Reception until this Trixie arrived and whisked me off to her office. There she introduced me to Timothy, the photographer, and a massive bloke called Ed, who turned out to be the producer of what he called the *Dreams Come True Extravaganza*.

He looked me up and down and said: 'No, no, no, Jim. This really won't do. Where's your clarinet?'

I said no one had told me to bring it.

'But we have to shoot you *in situ* and in character, with the clarinet. And not in those smart clothes. Trixie, get on to wardrobe. We want, item, cloth cap. Item, old mac. Item, grimy boots. Item, one piece string. ASAP, so that we can catch the last of the watery sun.'

And that's how I looked on the poster. Like some tramp from the 1930s. They stuck me outside the Festival Hall, cloth cap at my feet (which were inside the item grimy boots), with this dirty old mac tied round me middle with string. I looked like I should have been up before the beak for flashing. They didn't have a clarinet to spare, so Trixie was sent up the Charing Cross Road to buy one, while Timothy set up his lights ASAP so that he could catch the last of the watery sun. He shot three rolls of film and I never got to play a note. Fifty yards upstream, on my normal pitch, I could have earned twenty or thirty quid in that time.

After all that there was another bit of a lull. Trixie wrote to me and told me the date for the concert was fixed – 21st April, to kick off a new series of *Dreams Come True*. Then she sent me the names of the numbers Dr Marcus and Sara had selected from the list I'd sent in. Nothing difficult. Nothing I couldn't play in my sleep, except *They're Changing Guard at Buckingham Palace*, which someone had marked *alla marcia*.

No matter. I practised the numbers regularly. Played them while I was busking for a week or two. But they didn't bring in much money, so I was mightily relieved one night when Sara made what was now a rare visit and told me not to play anything that was going to be in the concert as it was all supposed to be a surprise.

'The posters are up,' she said. 'Have people been coming

up to you, saying that they recognised you?'

'Not a soul,' I said. 'I look different without the dirty mac.'

'They will,' she said. 'Especially those that watch on TV. You'll be in close up a lot of the time.' She gave me a big smile. 'The famous Bill Emms.'

I said: 'Jim. Jim Emms.'

I don't think she heard. She just went on talking. 'By the way, Marcus would like you to come in for a rehearsal the day before. For a run through with just a piano. In case there are any little problems to be ironed out. And you can go to wardrobe and get kitted out at the same time.'

'Fine,' I said.

But it wasn't. Afternoon of 20th April I go back to Capital Studios – with me clarinet, this time. Wait in Reception. Along comes Trixie. Off we go to this room somewhere down in the basement. And there's Dr Marcus and a piano and a pianist and a music stand and a whole sheaf of music.

'What's that?' I said.

'It's your music,' said Dr Marcus.

'What for? I know all the tunes by heart.'

'Yes,' he said. 'But I've done a concert arrangement for the Medley. Basically, you play the tunes, but you have to know how and where to come in, and there are some bits where you play variations. Nothing too difficult. It's straightforward enough. I hope,' and he gave a little laugh.

I looked at the music. 'It may well be straightforward to you,' I said, 'but it's Double Dutch to me.'

The penny dropped. 'You don't read?' said Dr Marcus.

'Not music,' I said. 'And who's Alla Marcia when she's at home?'

Conster-bloody-nation. Phone calls to Sara, to Big Ed, to a dozen people. Talk about the power of music to touch the emotions. I don't believe one clarinettist has ever made so many people so unhappy so fast. Along came Sara. Along came Big Ed. Along came one Rod, and three more Sarahs with two 'H's between them. Rows, arguments, recriminations, though they were all agreed on one thing…the whole evening was ruined. The *Dreams Come True* Orchestra couldn't play without music, yours truly couldn't play from music.

'But they're professional musicians,' I said. 'Can't they improvise?' Apparently not. 'Well, they wouldn't last five minutes as buskers,' I said. 'Punters come up with requests. You don't really know the tune. Not properly. So you play the bits you know and fake the rest. Jazz-bos call it "improvising". I call it faking.'

It was Sara who sorted everything out. 'Right,' she said. 'What we need is a Band of Buskers.'

And that's what we got. Trixie was sent out to buy a brand new A-to-Z of London, and I marked all the prime busking pitches on it. She spent all that evening and the following morning trawling around and by two o'clock on the afternoon of the concert the *Deams Come True* Strolling Players assembled on the stage of the Festival Hall. Two trumpets, one violin, one banjo, one mouth organ, and fourteen soprano saxes. Not quite what Dr Marcus had in mind.

Meanwhile, down in wardrobe, another panic was on. Twenty buskers and only two dirty old macs. Big Ed said they'd have to buy another eighteen dirty old macs. Sara said you couldn't buy dirty old macs. In the end Trixie was told to buy eighteen new macs and get them dirty in time for the dress rehearsal run through at three. One of the soprano sax players said he'd guarantee to get at least one mac very dirty in five minutes if Trixie would hang around, but I didn't think that was very nice.

Three o'clock comes. We're all on stage...*inside* the Festival Hall. Lights, wires, cameras, mikes, blokes in baseball caps all over the place. Dreams Come True Orchestra at their desks.

'Now,' said Big Ed. 'We've got two hours to get this London Medley sorted out.' He was looking to me to be the leader.

'Fine,' I said.

What he didn't tell me was that an hour and a half of those precious two hours would be taken up getting the sound balance right and deciding where to put the mikes. I suppose they've not done much work with fourteen soprano saxes at the Festival Hall. Anyway, round about a quarter to five we finally got down to a proper run-through.

And, as far as I was concerned, it was smashing. Great wall of sound. Melodies floating through. The place positively shaking with *vibrato*. *Obligatos* galore. I couldn't understand the sour faces that gathered round us when we finally ground to a halt.

The upshot of it all was that we were slung out. Oh, they compensated us financially. At first Trixie said we'd have to send invoices and within sixty days of the receipt of the invoices we'd get cheques in the post. But buskers don't want cheques, and one of the trumpet players said he wasn't leaving the stage without cash in hand right now. Poor little Trixie was sent off with eight bits of plastic to draw £2000 out of the nearest cash machine. Oh, and we were all offered free tickets to the actual show. I got the impression it hadn't exactly been a sell-out.

Then Sara took me to one side. She was trying to be nice about the whole thing. Full of apologies. In the background I could hear the lead clarinet from the Dreams Come True Orchestra playing my part as they ran through the London Medley while she talked to me. She said something about 'perhaps we hadn't thought the thing through properly.'

To be honest, I hadn't thought about it at all. 'How do you mean?' I said.

'I'm sorry, Bill,' she said. 'We're going to have to cancel. We can't have fourteen people's dreams coming true,' she said. 'The whole point of the show's to make *one* person special, to create a new celebrity. You can't have a whole crowd of new celebrities, not mass produced, all at once. That's no use to us.'

'But I can still give 'em a good show,' I said.

'It's not about being *good*,' she said. 'It's about being famous.'

I still didn't understand, couldn't see why she was angry. Broken dreams? These things happen every day. But I gave her a little kiss on the cheek as I handed over my dirty old mac, and we parted the best of friends.

But I didn't go to the concert. I spent the evening outside the Festival Hall, which was where I was playing at the time. *Outside* the Festival Hall.

The Critic's Tale

The Evil Transcribers

I'm not popular. That doesn't concern me in the slightest. I've never set out to be popular. At Westminster I was voted "The Most Unpopular Boy in School" three years running. At Cambridge… well, let's just say the world didn't exactly put itself out beating a path to my door, though a couple of Jesus jocks did smash it in one vulgar night. But that's fine by me – because the world is made up of average people, and the average person is a complete and utter waste of time. The average person should be forced to wear a T shirt with a government warning: 'Socialising with the wearer of this garment may damage your brain'.

"For me there can be no ease in human society… I must live completely alone and can creep into society only as absolutely necessary, I must live like an outcast…" You recognize the quotation, of course – Beethoven's *Heiligenstadt Testament* of 1802. Only, for me, it's not a question of "*must* live like an outcast". I *choose* to live as an outcast. And, to be quite honest, I haven't much time for Beethoven. Somewhat overrated as a composer, in my opinion.

And *my* opinion matters. That's not bragging. It's a fact. I'm a critic, a music critic. Oh dear, I know what you think, and, to be frank, I am wearied by your thoughts. I don't care that you don't like critics, but I do care that you almost certainly don't understand the function of criticism. You see my role in life as reacting to creativity. I see it as creativity itself. Let me explain how it works.

A new work is unveiled – a piece of music, of sculpture, of theatre. You listen, you look, you applaud. But without me you haven't the slightest idea what you are applauding. Not until I direct your attention to the strength of the new work. I forge the interplay between composer and audience. And without this creative role of the critic, music simply wouldn't move forward. We would be stuck in the sub-Brahmsian, neo-Tchaikovskian world of film scores and West End musicals. A world that devotes its time and resources to seeking to breathe new life into rotting corpses.

Because the worst enemies of musical progress are composers themselves. They delight in reworking old themes – variations on a theme by Purcell, Couperin, Haydn. Or in transcribing existing works for different ensembles. Think of the hours Brahms, Busoni, Liszt and Gounod – even Schoenberg – wasted re-working Bach organ pieces for violin and piano, voice and piano, chamber orchestra. Which brings to mind another critic… Albert Schweitzer. Not the brightest man in the world, but at least he had the intelligence to condemn Bach's own transcription of the *C Minor Concerto for Two Violins* into a piece for harpsichord. For so doing, Schweitzer rightly accused Bach of joining 'the evil transcribers'.

All of which brings me, rather neatly, to last night's concert at the Festival Hall. No, I am not writing yet another 'piece' for *The Custodian*. Certainly not. I am simply telling you what happened, because nobody else will listen!

I sat in the Foyer Bar, sipping what passes for red wine and watching the audience arrive. I knew there wouldn't be enough of them to fill the house, but there they were – brave souls who had come to wend their way through nearly two hours of music. I knew they'd manage to sit quietly for the first offering – Gustav Mahler's arrangement for orchestra of Schubert's 14th string quartet, *Death and the Maiden*. Very pretty. Very easy on the ear. And I knew most of them would stay awake for the concert *finale* – Anthony Payne's completion of Elgar's untidy sketches for his *Third Symphony* – although I cannot for the life of me see the point in creating something that's three quarters of a century past its "best before" date. Not when Elgar's *First Symphony* was already old fashioned when he wrote it in 1908… how did Beecham describe it? Ah yes – 'the musical equivalent of the towers of St Pancras station… neo-Gothic, you know.'

It was the piece in the middle that I was interested in, though I expected it to confound those around me. Jason Fitzroy's *Beyond Comprehension*. Rather a witty title, I thought, for a brand new BBC, Arts Council, Sony Corporation, Scottish Widows and-all-stations-to-the-*Credit Mutuel* commission. I know Jason quite well, we were contemporaries at Westminster and Cambridge. When we went up together, I was initially worried that he would start 'hanging around'. But he read Law while I read Music, and our paths never really crossed. I don't know when music became his 'thing', but in the last ten years a considerable amount of fuss has been made of him as a composer. *Why* this should be still eludes me.

I had a second glass of wine and flicked through the concert programme. Now, the notes were written by Ellen Latimer, another Cambridge contemporary. She'd produced some gushing prose about the Mahler/Schubert and the Payne/Elgar backed by reams of decidedly Internet standard research (I smelt Wikipedia), but had really gone to town about Jason's *oeuvre*. New textures, new forms and structures, new directions... new bed companions, I shouldn't wonder. If *Beyond Comprehension* was half as good as she described it, we were all in for an exciting seventeen and a half minutes.

They began to sound the gong and I hauled myself up to Level 3. Five minutes later we were all in the throes of *Death and the Maiden*. Over-ripe, over-written, over-scored, over-played... but at least, eventually over... mercifully.

There was a lot of moving about on stage before Jason's piece. Most of the string section disappeared, to be replaced by huge reinforcements in the percussion department. I prayed that we were not to be subjected to some poly-rhythmic extravangaza, incorporating salsa, jazz and *homage à Edmundo Ros*. That is not the way forward. "Borrowing" never solved any problem – financial or artistic. I thought of Milhaud and Bernstein and shuddered.

The conductor returned, the audience pulled itself together, and off we went. Seventeen and a half minutes later, we reached the finishing post with a sustained major chord from the brass and a *fortissimo* tattoo from the percussion that reminded me of the worst excesses of the Cuban Revolution.

I make a habit of not giving way to emotion normally, but this was a very special occasion. I rose to my feet, filled my lungs with the after-shave-and-perfumed air emanating from my neighbours, and booed as loudly as I could. But my boos were drowned by what, incredibly, appeared genuine enthusiasm from the masses. Jason had scored a veritable hit. They liked it, though 'why' was to me literally *Beyond Comprehension*. We had been down Memory Lane. It wasn't exactly *schmaltzy*, but it was unforgivably accessible, and I needed a drink.

I fought my way through the jolly suburban sybarites to the Mezzanine bar on Level 6 and ordered a large whisky. Ellen Latimer was there, and she suggested we went backstage to congratulate Jason.

'To congratulate him on what?' I said. 'His *new* direction?'

'You didn't like it?'

'What was there to like?' I said. 'At least when Schliemann took his bucket and spade to Troy and Carter took his jemmy to Thebes, they were digging up something the world didn't know about. This piece... the vein was exhausted decades ago!' I gulped my whisky and made a mental note to rework the Troy/Thebes analogy in my review.

Ellen smiled, rather condescendingly, I thought. 'You haven't studied the score, have you?'

I smiled back at the bitch. 'Music,' I said, 'is primarily for listening to, not looking at. Plenty of time for us to see how Jason has obtained his effect later, once we have established that he has achieved an effect.'

She kept the smile on her face. 'So, it's the first time you've heard it. It's wrong of me to expect you to get hold of it first go.'

I was furious. How dare she! I had heard everything there was to hear in Jason's offering – the early touches of Maxwell Davies, the quotations from Percy Grainger, the full frontal acknowledgement of Charles Ives.

'Get hold of it!' I said. 'For the rest of the evening I shall be struggling to get rid of it. Petty, tune-infested, riddled with emotion… my God, it was like Eric Coates on speed.' I made another mental note, to include the simile in my piece for *The Custodian*. Then I looked her square in her blue eyes. 'Are you sleeping with him?'

She put her hand on my arm. I had not invited her to.

'I thought *Beyond Comprehension* was pretty good for a Law graduate,' she said. 'I know one or two MA Mus guys who could never rise to such heights of creativity. And now, if you will excuse me, I'm off to congratulate Jason.' And she walked away.

I don't think I have ever been so angry, and I didn't like the feeling. How dare she walk off! After such a cheap jibe. And I had the perfect riposte. Dr Johnson's remark when some fool said a critic should be able to do the action he criticizes: 'Why, no, sir, this is not just reasoning… You may scold a carpenter who has made you a bad table, though you cannot make a table. It is not your trade to make tables.' I wanted to shout it after her. To shout it to the whole room. Very disconcerting.

It was clear that I was in no condition to sit through the digitally re-mastered Elgar, so I didn't return to the Hall, but started to head for home. I knew it wouldn't matter if I missed the second half of the concert, though just for a second an image from *Citizen Kane* did pass through my head. No problem then for me to write a couple of paragraphs on the orchestra's performance of the alleged *Third Symphony* without having to sit through it.

Then I thought – why go home? Why not sit down and write my review there and then, while the rage was hot within me, while my mind had the keen edge of contempt?

I collected my bag from the cloakroom, went back up to the Mezzanine, ordered another whisky, found a chair overlooking the Thames, and settled down with my laptop.

It wasn't easy to get started. For one thing, there was this confounded street musician down by the river. Faint, but irritating. Playing what I suppose he would have called *Hits from Carmen* on his clarinet. Not helpful.

And the laptop was annoying me. It just sat there, like some demanding pet, wanting to be played with. A blank screen with that mocking, empty look. All those unused keys. And it was so infernally hot in the room. By the time the bloody street musician got to the *Habanera* from Act I of *Carmen*, I needed another drink.

With it came inspiration. It seemed to me that there was an exact parallel between Jason's *oeuvre* and the clarinetist's miserable efforts. Trivial – they were both trivial pursuits. Travesties of what they should have been. Both were vulgar, cheap, shoddy derivatives. Superficial – a waste of other people's talent… Bizet's in the case of the street musician, the LPO's in the case of Jason. 'Glib', that was the precise word that summed up the whole seventeen and a half minutes' worth of drivel. I wanted to let fly. Words like 'sloppy', 'sentimental', and especially 'superficial' surged into my mind. But I resisted them. I was aware that I'd had a drink or two and needed to be on my guard.

But even as my fingers stabbed at the keyboard, I knew that what I was writing was good. I began with a reference to the street musician, setting the scene. I went on to draw the parallel between the street musician and the streetwalker. "For one thing is certain," I wrote, "last night at the Festival Hall, Jason Fitzroy prostituted the talent that has been claimed for him. Out of this young lion of British contemporary music came forth sweetness… sweetness to saturate the taste-buds and clog the palette." I even had a title for my piece. Knowing how fond of puns they are at *The Custodian*, I decided I'd give them my own play on words, so I called my review: *Not Beyond Criticism*.

It flowed. And the odd thing was, the very weakness of Jason's music seemed to give strength to my writing. It was, without doubt, the best thing I had ever written. I checked that there had been no unforeseen slip-ups with the Elgar, e-mailed my review to the paper, had a nightcap when I got home, and fell into bed, tired but pleased with myself.

In the morning, I was the one that phoned *The Custodian* – it was not the other way round. I have heard some of the stories circulating, but, let's get this straight, *I* phoned *them*. To find out what the hell they were playing at. It wasn't just a re-working of my piece that they had printed, it was a travesty. It flatly contradicted what I had written. Jason's *oeuvre* was 'a witty new direction for music…' One that combined 'respect for traditional music form' with 'daring innovations and a charming light-heartedness'. And so on and so on and so on… *ad* bloody *nauseam*. It simply wasn't what I had written. Not one word.

So I phoned Giles at the office. Asked him what was going on. His answer took my breath away. He said my piece was 'unusable'. He said he'd been at the concert and he'd heard *Beyond Comprehension*.

I could tell from his voice that, like Ellen, he'd enjoyed Jason's limp offering, but I reminded him that he was bound by the Code of the Critic and the Ethics of Journalism to respect – and to print – my opinion. No matter how much we disagreed about the artistic merit of a performance, a piece of music, or even a contralto's hair-style, my view had to prevail.

Do you know what he said?

It wasn't my "opinion" that concerned him. It was my style!... which he labelled as between seventy and a hundred years out of date. He said it was "wordy… contrived… smacked of Cardus at his most laborious… nodded in the direction of GBS, but lacked the warmth of Irish wit… more suited to the *Morning Post* of the 1920s than *The Custodian* of today…" When I refuted every point he made, he began to bluster, to lose his temper, and he ended up calling my piece "verbose, yet glib", "snooty, yet vulgar", "pretentious, but cheap".

We ended the conversation on bad terms, with Giles recommending that I shouldn't bother to submit any more reviews. The partnership was over. Then he slammed the phone down. Note that, if you will. *He* slammed the phone down, not me.

For I am not an emotional person. Emotion does not trouble me. And neither does popularity. But I do have one regret about the events of that evening at the Festival Hall. I just wish that, when I looked into Ellen's blue eyes and she put her hand on my arm, the moment had lasted a little longer, and that she had not turned so hastily and walked away quite so quickly.

The Nerd's Tale

Toscanini's Foot

Yes, all right. I admit it. I'm a nerd. That is, *I* don't think I'm a nerd, but that's what all my friends call me. Well, that's what Paul calls me, and he's my best mate. OK, OK, my *only* mate. Yeah, yeah, yeah… all right… I can't really talk about *all* my friends. If I had a whole lot of friends, I wouldn't be a nerd, would I?

It's all about computers, of course. I'm good with computers. And most of the people I come across seem to look down on you if you're good with computers. Well, I've got news for them. I look down on people who *aren't* good with computers. I can't understand them any more than they can understand me. Why buy a computer if you're not going to make real use of it? The software these days… the programmes… fantastic, beautiful. They can change your life. They changed mine.

I first heard about the Toscanini thing from Paul. We were at school together back in the late 80s, and we've sort of kept in touch ever since. Never mind me, Paul's weird. He doesn't appreciate computers. He's got one, a good one, but it's a mess. There's no system in the way he orders it, and I reckon he uses just about one thousandth of its power… if that. Every time I go round to his place I show him better ways to access his files – real kid's stuff – but he says I do it all too quickly, and that I'd make a lousy teacher, and, anyway, he'd rather talk about something else.

But it was me that Paul turned to about the Toscanini thing, because he knows I'm good. He phoned me up long before it happened, saying he wanted to talk to me about a really exciting project. All to do with Toscanini, which at the time I reckoned was an opera or something. But Paul explained that Toscanini was a famous conductor, 'back in the days before they had computers', was the way he put it. 'B.C.' It's a kind of joke he makes at my expense. I don't mind. One day, when I've got time, I'll think of a joke at *his* expense.

So Paul told me all about Toscanini, and how they'd found this piece of film in the archives down in the vaults of what used to be the NBC in New York. Apparently there was a time when Toscanini worked for the NBC. He conducted their orchestra. And it was an old piece of film, shot in the 1940s or 1950s, Paul reckoned. It was unique, he said, because it was shot with just a single camera, head on, focused on Toscanini himself, face on, from the back of the orchestra. It was filmed while he was conducting the overture to an opera called *Aida*. I'm not usually good with music, but I know that piece now. Well, I couldn't help getting to know it, the amount of time I worked on it. Not great, is it? I don't go in for Egyptian music. I like Elgar. He knew how to write. I'm very fond of the *Enigma Variations* – especially that bit they call *Nimrod*. That's three minutes and twenty-one seconds of very nice listening indeed. That's as good as anything from Barry Manilow or Chris de Burgh or Charlotte Church. Anyway, the thing was, what mattered to Paul about this bit of film was that it had Toscanini conducting the overture to *Aida*. Because, Paul said, that was the music of the first big breakthrough in Toscanini's career. He was deputy conductor at some Brazilian opera house way back, and the proper conductor fell sick one night, so the teenage Toscanini leapt in and conducted the entire opera from memory.

Now that did impress me. I don't say the young Toscanini had a memory to compare with my smallest laptop, even, but I guess storing an opera score in your brain must take up quite a few 'k'. I've got a machine in the office – an RX16 – that could hold the score of every opera that's ever been written like a pea in a bucket. And you could access the scores in so many ways. You want to know how many F#s in Mozart? Click. There you are. Would you like to know how many bars rest there are in the works of Beethoven? Click. There's the answer. I told Paul, but he didn't seem impressed. He said no one would be interested in how many bars rest there were in Beethoven. I said that wasn't the point. I said the point was you could find out. The information was there. And he just laughed and said I was an anorak. Which I'm not. I'm a nerd, and proud of it.

He wasn't interested because he just wanted to go on about Toscanini and this bit of film. He said the outfit he was working for... Did I tell you about that? Well, it's something to do with putting on concerts. Paul has explained it to me, but he always picks the wrong time, like the system's just gone down, or I'm looking at some new software, or there's a glitch of some kind. Yes, I know, computers aren't perfect. What is in this world? People think cars are great, and they're always breaking down. Yet that doesn't stop people thinking cars are great. But the second there's any glitch with a computer, people want to trash the whole system. They don't understand. Computers are beautiful things, really beautiful things. And I don't think it's going too far to say they're man's best friend.

But I mustn't get sidetracked. I was telling you about Paul and Toscanini, right? Paul's outfit had decided to promote a concert. It was going to celebrate some centenary or other, something about Toscanini's first appearance in New York or Milan or somewhere. And it was going to be a big affair. There was going to be not just one concert, but half a dozen – all taking place simultaneously, all over the world… Paris, Milan, Berlin, New York, Rio de Janeiro and right here in London. At the Festival Hall.

And Toscanini was going to conduct them all. And that was where I came in. The idea was to project the old film of Toscanini onto a glass screen in all six concert halls, facing all six orchestras. All this was going to be synchronized, so all six orchestras would be playing at exactly the same time to the same conductor at exactly the same speed – which Paul insisted on calling *tempo*. He said it would be a unique opportunity to assess the relative playing of each orchestra on a single piece of music. It was like a sort of competition. And all the concerts were going to be recorded, and televised live. And the idea was to cut from one orchestra to another. And afterwards, a CD would be issued of all the orchestras playing this overture – which sounded to me like a complete waste of time, but Paul insisted it was a truly international event.

So where did I come in? Well, they wanted to enhance

the image of Toscanini, add colour, sharpen it up, flesh it out, that sort of thing… using computers. People like Paul talk about 'using computers' as though it was like using a set of spanners. I tried to explain to him that you don't need computer*s*, all you need is *a* computer and the right software. But he was getting too excited, and he asked if it was possible to produce a back view of Toscanini, so that while the orchestra saw his face, the audience would see his back, just like they would at a real concert, all projected on to this glass screen, just as though the guy was still alive and right there.

Well, of course that's possible. And I started to explain how it was possible, but Paul couldn't – or more likely *wouldn't* take it in. I think his trouble is, he spends too much time with people. So I gave up and asked him what other music these orchestras were going to play that night. And he said he'd no idea what Paris and Rio and that lot were doing – that was up to them – but at the Festival Hall it was going to be an All Italian Evening. Apparently, *Aida*'s Italian, not Egyptian. Well, I don't like Italian music either, unless you count Dean Martin. But Paul went on and on about a whole string of names like Nero, and Bono, and Bleriot… people I'd never heard of.

I said, was Toscanini going to conduct all those, too? And Paul said, no, not unless there were some more surprises in the NBC vaults. No, conducting the rest of the Festival Hall concert was going to be down to some young Italian whose name was Vittorio Callendrini or something. Never heard of him? No, neither had I.

The next three months were an absolute joy as far as I was concerned. Paul got me a disk of the film which disappointingly turned out to be of very poor quality. It looked to me as though it had been shot during a dust storm from the look of it. There he was, this weird-looking geek, bit of a nerd himself I reckoned – white hair flopping, shoulders hunched… He had that very bad posture that you can get if you spend too much time on a computer without a break. I make sure that I get up from my desk and turn round at least once every three hours and stretch my arms out four times each. And while we're talking about arms, this Toscanini's arms were a real challenge. Producing a back view so that we could flip the image round was straightforward enough, once I'd programmed it all in, though I do have to say that it took a lot of time, of course, and was not particularly exciting. But the arms! I tried to explain to Paul what I had to do, but he wasn't interested. People never are. They love the result, but they never want to know how you achieved it. That's the reason why they think anyone who really knows how to tap into the real power of the computer is a nerd. The problem is people just won't learn. Oh, it's great, they say. Fantastic! Incredible! They talk like they're looking at a firework display or a magic show. They won't listen to what I say because I'm talking about science, not art, and being science there should be no mystery about it. Everyone should understand how it works.

But what's the point? The Pauls of this world will never understand computers, and people like me will always be nerds in their eyes. To him, what mattered were the results… which were good. There was Toscanini - front and back, and I'd put him in colour, crystal clear, no dust storm – starting the orchestra off on this *Aida*.

The next thing Paul wanted to know was, would I be there on the night, in the Festival Hall, 'working' the computer? I told Paul, you don't 'work' a computer, any more than you 'work' a TV or a radio. I started to explain the process, and, again, he didn't want to know. But I said yes, I'd make sure it was all right on the night, and he booked me in.

The rehearsal went well. I checked that everything was OK technically, and Paul explained it all to the orchestra. I could see most of them didn't understand, and there were some who weren't taking it seriously. But then we switched on, and there was Toscanini and they all shut up. Of course, I'd brushed out everything else on the film, so Toscanini was on his own. The stage hands moved the dais up and down till his feet were on it, and I adjusted the image on the glass screen till it was life size. There was some expert on Toscanini there who knew everything about him: how tall he was, what he ate, where he bought his clothes, all his mannerisms, likes and dislikes. A real bore. I tried to explain to him how I'd dealt with Toscanini's hair, but he simply wasn't interested.

Anyway, we ran the programme through, with the soundtrack from the original film, just so the orchestra could see how it worked and could follow what they had to do. Then we ran it again, only this time with no soundtrack and with the orchestra playing.

Paul got so excited. He kept talking about 'dynamics' and 'fervour' and 'intensity', and how this was the first time Toscanini had conducted in over fifty years. I said something about, well, you'll be in trouble if the audience want an *encore*, which I thought was a pretty good joke, but

I didn't hear anyone laugh. People never listen to nerds.

The orchestra had a second go, and a third, and the leader discussed bits of it with them, and there was a lot of nodding and a couple of sulks from the woodwind, and a stupid trombonist said something about 'dead man waving', which they did laugh at, but in general they all went along with it.

After a couple of hours, Vittorio whatever-his-name-was, the guy who was going to conduct the rest of the concert, arrived, and the screen was hauled up to the roof, and they started rehearsing the other pieces.

Paul was thrilled, and he patted me on the back and told me what a great job I'd done. I started to explain how simple it was really, but he said he'd got to talk to New York and Paris and Milan to see how they were doing.

So I thought I'd just tinker with the programme once more, because I'd noticed a bit where Toscanini's foot needed moving a fraction. His balance didn't look right. It was too late to do anything about it for the other venues, but I thought I might as well get it perfect for London. It turned out to be quite a tricky job, but I got it done with more than ten minutes to spare. I've no idea why Paul got so ratty about it… biting his nails and muttering something about 'why couldn't people leave good things alone…' But I think it's important to make people see just what a powerful machine is capable of. When I'd finished, Paul relaxed a bit and asked if I wanted a sandwich, which, of course, I didn't. I'm not interested in eating and drinking. I think it's a waste of time.

The audience were coming in. We were up in the Control Room, watching on CCTV. Big event. Sold out.

Paul had shown me one of the posters. Good. Well, all right, though it was all about Toscanini – nothing about the software involved. Didn't even mention what computer I'd been using.

Orchestra comes on, then the leader. I said to Paul 'why doesn't the leader come on first, then they could all play "Follow Me Leader"?' But he didn't laugh, because he hadn't bothered to listen. People don't. Not when they reckon you're a nerd. Down comes the screen. Paul gets the signal from the leader on stage that all was ready. He checked that all the other cities were standing by, I hit ENTER, and Toscanini appeared on the screen. Freeze frame. We'd agreed on a ten second freeze before Toscanini raised his baton. Paul said we needed that for the audience to grasp what was happening, and get over their surprise.

I could hear Paul behind me, counting down the seconds like Toscanini was a rocket about to take off. And when Toscanini raised his arms and brought the orchestra in, Paul gave a suppressed yell of 'Yes!' And the orchestra started. Paul checked with Paris and the other places and everything was going fine. I told him I knew it would be, but people always expect computers will let them down. And he patted me on the shoulder again and said that there were over 100 million people in Europe alone watching, and wasn't that incredible?

Now, I admit, when we got to the bit where I'd shifted Toscanini's foot, there was a slight glitch, and for a second or two, he moved in a series of rapid jerks. That happens from time to time. It's not a big problem, and I could have sorted it out. It would simply have been a matter of stopping the programme, restoring the original, and then re-booting. It would have been simply a question of going back to the beginning and starting again. And I tried to explain that to Paul, but he just *wouldn't* listen. Why is it no one's ever interested in how computers work?

Anyway, I stopped the programme and Toscanini froze. But the orchestra kept on playing. And Vittorio What's-his-name leapt on to the stage and started conducting. From memory.

They never gave me a chance. And why was it such a big deal? Apparently, it worked fine in Paris and Milan and everywhere else. But people never remember when computers get things right. They only remember when things go wrong.

Except people like me. Except nerds.

THE
CONCERTGOER'S TALE

Spell-Bound Love

I thought she'd be there. No, I *knew* she'd be there. In a way, I feared she'd be there. But whether I bought my ticket just to see if I was right, or because I wanted to confront her and show her that she didn't mean anything to me... I still don't know.

When I went online at www.southbankcentre.co.uk to buy the ticket, it was obvious there'd be a lot of people there. Almost all the really cheap seats had been taken. The choir seats were sold out. They used to be our favourites... when we were together... before it all got "out of tune" (her stupid phrase, not mine). She did all the talking, all the labelling, all the fault finding when it came to splitting up. I did all the crying, and I'll never forgive her for that.

I stared at the screen on my laptop, at all those "unavailable seats", wondering which one she'd booked to park her pretty little arse on. Then I thought, the best I could do, the seats where I had the best chance of 'accidentally' bumping into her, would be the Side Seats, and that would only work if I knew which side of the Choir she'd be in. All that mattered, to start with, was that I didn't make myself obvious, didn't sit somewhere where *she* could spot *me*. So the best place would be the Balcony, back of the Hall,

Level 6. You can see the whole of the auditorium from the Balcony, and, yeah, OK, it's mainly the backs of people's heads, but since she was most likely to be in the Choir seats - because she'd have marked down the concert long before I did... she was always way ahead of me in organising our cultural life - she'd be sitting behind the orchestra, facing me.

I clicked on N11 and booked it. Nice, safe seat in the very back row. She'd never see me there, and that gave her no chance of taking evasive action. I knew that one glance at me and she'd be off, Fifth Symphony of Sibelius or no Fifth Symphony of Sibelius. That was the concert closer, you see. Three works written in 1915: Respighi's *The Fountains of Rome*, de Falla's *El amor brujo*, and then the Sibelius. Oh, how she loved that symphony. I wouldn't call it "our song". It was never that. You can't have a symphony as "our song". No, Sibelius's Fifth belongs to her, to my Naomi. And she's still *my* Naomi, whatever she says. The Symphony belongs to *her*, but *she* belongs to me... or should do.

She introduced me to Sibelius's Fifth. She was barmy about it. She said it was the sexiest piece of music ever written. She made me listen to it. Didn't say anything about it, just told me to listen. That was very early on in our relationship, long before I got into her knickers. She sat me down on her sofa, shoved a glass of wine in my fist, and clicked the remote. I wanted her to snuggle up beside me, but she wouldn't. She wanted me to listen. I leaned back against the cushions, and tried to pull her down gently beside me. But she didn't want that. She wanted to listen. She sat forward, round-shouldered, head cocked at an angle, like a bird, intense.

When the music stopped, she turned to me, her face deadpan, and she said: 'Whatcha think of that?'

I didn't have to lie. I thought it was good. So I said: 'I *really* liked it', and I meant it.

Then she said: 'What did it make you feel?'

I didn't have an answer for that. It was just a great piece of music. But I nodded my head, and said: 'Good. It made me feel good.'

That made her sit bolt upright. 'Good? In what way "good"?'

It was like I was being interrogated, like I'd done something wrong, and it took me by surprise. 'OK,' I said. 'What did it make *you* feel?'

The cork flew out of the bottle. I can't remember everything she said, but I do remember she said something about 'being brought to the edge of an orgasm again and again'. It made her feel horny, made her feel that she was hard at it, that her body was being wound up, that she was heading for the world's biggest orgasm. Again and again, apparently. She was most explicit. 'But,' she said, 'Sibelius is such a bastard. He just won't let you go that last bit. He keeps denying you that moment of ecstatic release. Just winds you up, again and again.'

She sat there, staring at me, eyes flashing, body erect, with the palms of her hands turned towards me, as though she was offering me those feelings. And when she did that, I didn't need any Sibelius to get horny, too. Couldn't wait to get inside her knickers.

'Play it again,' I said, and I smiled, to make it like a joke. I felt I needed to make a joke to re-establish myself in the conversation.

She laughed. And five minutes later, we were in bed together. But she didn't have the world's biggest ever orgasm.

All the time we were together, her Ex was a presence. He shared her passion for Sibelius, and the two of them may well have shared the world's biggest ever orgasm… so far. I never asked. Didn't want to know. She told me her Ex was the one who'd introduced *her* to Sibelius's Fifth, and that made it seem that it was like some icy Olympic flame that was being passed from one lover to another… and had now come to me. Well, I haven't passed on Sibelius's Fifth. Haven't wanted to. Not because I didn't like it. I love it… *used to* love it, until the relationship with Naomi hit the rocks, or the iceberg, or whatever it was that sank the bloody thing. Who am I kidding? It was her Ex.

It was ten months ago that everything went pear-shaped. Her Ex came back, out of the shadows… I'm sure he did. It's the only thing that explains what happened. Naomi suddenly decided that we'd lost the art of talking to each other, that we had nothing new to say. Then she wanted to spend more time on her own. Yeah? Really? On her own? I don't think so. That was her Ex again. Then she lost her appetite for sex. Well, sex with me.

Within two months the relationship was as dead as a South Bank concrete walkway. She packed her bags and left. Big apology, but no tears as far as she was concerned. All she left behind was the smell of bad temper. It was as though she believed that *I'd* done something wrong. It was nothing to do with me, and all to do with her shitty Ex.

I was devastated. No forwarding address. And she was screening her calls, so I never got through to her. I left message after message. Bitch. Of course, there were no calls to me from her, just a couple of texts on the mobile, reminding me when the rent was due and hoping I was "all right". Bitch. There was no way of getting hold of her and telling her what I thought of her. Bitch. Bitch! I texted that one word to her so many times, but I never got any satisfaction from doing so, because she never replied. Which was why I wanted to find her, and why I booked that seat at the Festival Hall.

I was into the auditorium the moment they opened the doors. I went up to the back of the Balcony and stood there, trying to check out people as they came in. It would have helped if I'd had some clue as to what Naomi might be wearing - maybe something she'd bought while we were together. Christ knows I'd put in enough hours trudging round Monsoon and Next, with that bloody junk music pumping through the ceilings while Naomi tried on coats and sweaters and dresses, and I felt my brain turning to compost. There was that bright mohair sweater, a kind of ripple of blues. I used to like her in that. Really like her. Felt really chuffed to be seen with her when she wore that.

But even if she'd come in stark naked it would have been hard to spot her in that crowd. The Hall was filling quickly. I strained my eyes. There was a woman in the front row of the Choir who looked a bit like her, just for a moment. But then I thought, no, and I realised it was barmy searching for her until everyone was sitting down.

On came the orchestra, then the conductor, and we were into *The Fountains of Rome*. I didn't listen to any of it. I was angry with myself. The Balcony had been a stupid mistake. Too far away. But then I noticed that there were several empty seats, scattered throughout the Hall… in the Boxes, of course, but also in the Rear and Front Stalls, and a couple in the Choir. There was a chance that I could change my seat in the Interval, and grab a better one from which to scan the audience. But to be sure that a seat really was free, I'd have to wait until the break between *The Fountains of Rome* and *El amor brujo*, when they let the latecomers in.

I waited. The Respighi finished. A brief pause, and we were in the clutches of "Love the Magician". Good. Plenty of empty seats hadn't been filled, some at the end of rows, which meant I could wait till almost everyone was seated after the interval, and then slip in quickly.

Things hotted up with de Falla. I began to feel some kind of excitement. I was certain Naomi was in the Hall, and that I'd find her. My eyes were constantly raking the audience, section by section as the music swept on. Definitely not in the Choir. I switched my gaze to the left side. Nothing. The right side…

We were halfway through the *Ritual Fire Dance* when I saw her… side seats… on the right, on the brass side. Three things gave her away: the way that she was sitting… hunched forward, just like on the sofa, listening to Sibelius that first time; and the tilt of her head, like a child deep in thought; and, last of all, that mohair sweater. It was her! I felt sick with excitement. My gaze never left her. She wasn't going to get away now. The *Ritual Fire Dance* came to its crashing end with that fusillade of chords. Was she alone? I couldn't tell. There were guys sitting on either side of her. Well, they could sod off, that was where I should have been. Was one of them *with* her? I'd see about that later. But the good news was that there was an empty seat, just behind her. After the interval, that would be mine.

Plan. I had to have a plan. When the interval came, she'd either stay where she was or leave the Hall by the exit to Level 4. I'd make my way to the opposite side of the Hall, and leave by the exit to Level 6. Then I'd go down the stairs to Level 2, cross the Hall via the Foyer, wait for the end of interval gong, and then race up the stairs to Level 4 on Naomi's side. That would be the tricky bit, timing it so that I could be pretty certain that she'd gone back to her seat, but that there was still time for me to get to that empty seat behind her. I wanted to take her by surprise.

Now I was thinking… come on, come on, come *on*… get this bloody music over. But there was a whole lot more of de Falla until the cow singing the last song finally shut her mouth and the music came to an end.

Time to go. I forced my way along the row, banging into people's knees, half-tripping over their feet, generating a lot of anger. Who cares? Sod them all. I reached the aisle, but it was already blocked with people wanting early bloody drinks or ice creams. More pushing. More anger. There was a bloke who tried to push past me. I wanted to barge him over. I could have kicked an elderly couple who'd dropped their programme and brought everyone to a halt. I wanted to punch a bloke who suddenly came to a dead stop in the doorway. I didn't do any of those things. It was like bloody Sibelius and his suppressed orgasms…

I was finally out of the Hall and racing down the stairs. Fool, fool… I was going to get to the other side far too early at this rate. I slowed right down and a kid trod on my heel. Why do people take kids to concerts? Waste of time…

I reached the Foyer. There was time for a drink. I joined the queue, and waited and waited. Finally, I got to the bar and ordered a large glass of red wine. The guy took so long fetching it, I had to swig it down.

The gong started. I headed up the stairs… Level 3… Level 4… I climbed the last half flight slowly, until I was just high enough to see the lobby. No sign of Naomi. The last few people were just going into the auditorium. I joined them. The ushers were on the point of shutting the doors and didn't ask to see my ticket. I was in.

I took the seat quickly, in the row behind her, *directly* behind her. Couldn't have been better. She didn't turn round. She didn't know I was there. But I could see her and smell her and I could have touched her.

The music started. It was hot and stuffy in the Hall, and I was very slightly woozy from the wine. It was hard to concentrate. I couldn't look at the orchestra. I could only look at Naomi… at the back of her head, at her hair, at her neck… the great thing about that mohair sweater was that it was kind of loose, wide at the neck so that it almost slipped off her shoulders. I loved that. I sat there, gazing at her shoulders, thinking of the time we were together…

…the first dates, and the first sex… going to parties… the first night together… the first weekend, oh Christ… and setting up our own routines… our favourite *café*, favourite *delicatessen*, favourite pasta in our favourite *bistro*. And, no matter what she says, I thought the sex was fantastic. Then there was the fun of introducing each other to the films, the books, the paintings that we liked…

How was I to know it was only going to have the lifespan of a hamster? How was I to know she was going to end up sitting beside her Ex with me sitting behind her?

When the first movement ended, I whispered her name, very softly. She whirled round, saw me, made a face like I'd spat on her, and then turned her back on me. The music started up again. I couldn't help myself. I kept whispering her name. I thought about the weekend we'd had in Helsinki. God, I'd practically learned the Wikipedia article about Sibelius by heart… and spouted it all to her… and she'd been impressed. I'm sure she'd been impressed…

'Naomi, please…'

She whirled round again and mouthed 'Shut up'.

… the day we started living together… I'll never forget that… our first anniversary… lying in bed with her on a sunny Sunday morning, watching her while she was asleep…

I put out my hand and very gently, with the tips of my fingers, stroked her shoulder… just one stroke.

She didn't take any notice. I stroked her shoulder again. Still no notice. The symphony was nearing the end, that series of rising and plunging intervals on the horns. That was the bit she loved most of all.

I couldn't help myself. 'Naomi,' I said, so quietly that no one could have heard me but her, 'I love you… I love you… I just love you, that's all… Please…'

I went on saying 'please', in between each of the last chords. So quietly I swear no one else could have heard… not even her bloody Ex sitting beside her.

Boom! Boom! The symphony was over.

In that split second before the applause got going,

Naomi turned on me.

'I'm going to call the police!' She was furious. 'I want the police!' She was snarling. 'You're fucking mad! I want the police!' She pushed her way out of the seats. 'Fucking mad! I'm getting the police!' She was hysterical. Off she went, and I could see her talking to the ushers and pointing at me.

The bloke who'd been sitting next to her came up to me. 'She's right,' he said. 'You're a lunatic.'

'Oh yeah,' I said. 'And who are you? Her fucking Ex?'

'No,' he said. 'I'm a fucking music lover.'